NOV 2 4 2003

16

W9-AAJ-906

A Note to Parents and Caregivers:

Read-it! Joke Books are for children who are moving ahead on the amazing road to reading. These fun books support the acquisition and extension of reading skills as well as a love of books.

Published by the same company that produces *Read-it!* Readers, these books introduce the question/answer pattern that helps children expand their thinking about language structure and book formats.

When sharing a book with your child, read in short stretches, pausing often to talk about the pictures and the meaning of the book. The question/answer format works well for this purpose and provides an opportunity to talk about the language and meaning of the jokes. Have your child turn the pages and point to the pictures and familiar words. Read the story in a natural voice; have fun creating the voices of characters or emphasizing some important words. And be sure to reread favorite parts.

There is no right or wrong way to share books with children. Find time to read with your child, and pass on the legacy of literacy.

Adria F. Klein, Ph.D.
Professor Emeritus
California State University
San Bernardino, California

Managing Editor: Bob Temple
Creative Director: Terri Foley
Editors: Brenda Haugen, Nadia Higgins
Designer: John Moldstad
Page production: Picture Window Books
The illustrations in this book were prepared digitally.

Picture Window Books
5115 Excelsior Boulevard
Suite 232
Minneapolis, MN 55416
1-877-845-8392
www.picturewindowbooks.com

Printed in the United States of America.

Library of Congress Cataloging-in-Publication Data
Dahl, Michael.
Ding dong : a book of knock-knock jokes / written by Michael Dahl ;
illustrated by Ryan Haugen ; reading advisers, Adria F. Klein, Susan Kesselring.
p. cm. — (Read-it! joke books)
ISBN 1-4048-0235-5
1. Knock-knock jokes. I. Haugen, Ryan, 1972- II. Title.
PN6231.K55 D343 2003
818'.602—dc21
                                                        2003004871

Ding Dong

A Book of Knock-Knock Jokes

Michael Dahl • Illustrated by Ryan Haugen

Reading Advisers:
Adria F. Klein, Ph.D.
Professor Emeritus, California State University
San Bernardino, California

Susan Kesselring, M.A., Literacy Educator
Rosemount-Apple Valley-Eagan (Minnesota) School District

PICTURE WINDOW BOOKS
Minneapolis, Minnesota

Knock knock.
  Who's there?
Hi.
  Hi who?

Hi who! Hi who!
It's off to work we go!

Knock knock.
        Who's there?
Harry.
        Harry who?

6   Harry up, and answer the door!

Knock knock.
Who's there?
Tennis.
Tennis who?

	1	2	3	4	5
CHRIS	5	0	0	0	0
BETSY	5	0	0	0	0

10

Tennis five plus five! 7

Knock knock.
  Who's there?
Abby.
  Abby who?

8   Abby stung me on the nose.

Knock knock.
   Who's there?
Tori.
   Tori who?

Tori I bumped into you.

Knock knock.
    Who's there?
Zookeeper.
    Zookeeper who?

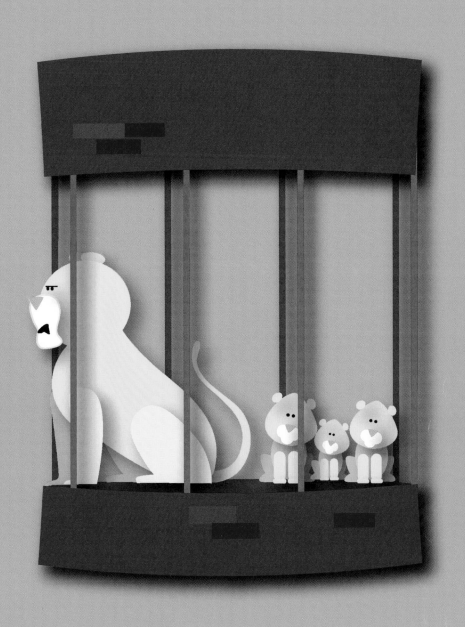

Zookeeper away from me! 11

Knock knock.
  Who's there?
Lena.
  Lena who?

Lena little closer,
       and I'll tell you.

Knock knock.
Who's there?
Lenny.
Lenny who?

Lenny give you a kiss.

Knock knock.
    Who's there?
Alaska.
    Alaska who?

14   Alaska my mom for an answer.

Knock knock.
    Who's there?
Pudding.
    Pudding who?

Pudding on your shoes
before your socks is a bad idea.   15

Knock knock.
  Who's there?
Pasta.
  Pasta who?

Pasta salt please.

Knock knock.
  Who's there?
Gopher.
  Gopher who?

Gopher help.
I'm stuck in the mud!

Knock knock.
  Who's there?
Gorilla.
  Gorilla who?

Gorilla cheese sandwich
for me please.

Knock knock.
Who's there?
Luke.
Luke who?

Luke before you leap.

Knock knock.
    Who's there?
Hugo.
    Hugo who?

Hugo jump in the lake!

Knock knock.
    Who's there?
Andrew.
        Andrew who?

Andrew on the wall,
and she is in trouble!

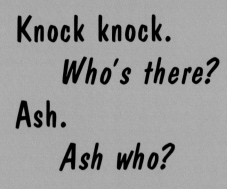

Knock knock.
      Who's there?
Ash.
      Ash who?

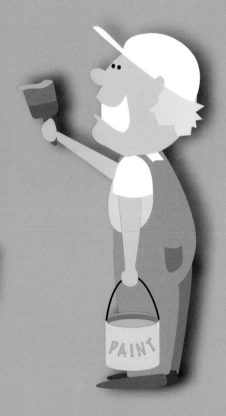

Ash sure could use some
help painting the house.